Jeffrey and the Fourth-Grade Ghost

Baseball Card Fever

Other
Jeffrey and the Fourth-Grade Ghost
Books

And
Jeffrey and the Third-Grade Ghost

Jeffrey and the Fourth-Grade Ghost

BOOK TWO

Baseball Card Fever

Megan Stine
AND
H. William Stine

FAWCETT COLUMBINE
NEW YORK

To Polly, Ira, and Andrew—
three cool cats who are strictly from
"best-friendsville"

Recommended for grades two to four

A Fawcett Columbine Book
Published by Ballantine Books
Copyright © 1989 by Cloverdale Press, Inc.

Library of Congress Catalog Card Number: 89-91685

ISBN: 0-449-90416-4

Text design by Mary A. Wirth
Illustrations by Marcy Ramsey

Manufactured in the United States of America
First Edition: September 1989
10 9 8 7 6 5 4 3

Chapter One

"Did you find them yet, Dad?" Jeffrey Becker asked for the eighth time in two minutes.

"Not yet," his father said. He blew a layer of dust off a carton, then looked up at Jeffrey. "And please stop asking me every fifteen seconds."

"No problem, Dad," said Jeffrey. He sat down on an old trunk and looked around the dark, dusty attic of his house. His dad had opened about fifty cartons already and he still hadn't found them!

Jeffrey made himself count up to thirty before he asked again, "Find them yet?"

Mr. Becker sighed heavily. "Just wait, Jeffrey."

Waiting was not one of Jeffrey's favorite activities. Especially now, when any minute his father was going to find the right box and take out his old collection of baseball cards! Exactly one hundred and thirteen of them—all in perfect condition and all of them at least thirty years old! They were the cards his father had bought or traded when he was a kid.

"I can't wait to show your cards to my friends," Jeffrey said. "Do you know what they'll do?"

"No, what? Do you think we should have an emergency medical team standing by?" Mr. Becker asked with a smile.

"Well, Ben will do some kind of scientific test on your cards to prove that they're really that old. But Ricky Reyes won't care about that. He'll just count them to be sure that he still has more cards than any of us. And Kenny will know which ones are the most valuable because he's been reading a book about old baseball cards."

Mr. Becker lifted another box from a stack of three. He set it on the floor. "What about Melissa?"

"Well, she'll look at them the longest. She'll check out every player's batting average. And after reading each one she'll say, 'Pretty good. But mine's better.' And Max . . . he's really going to flip out."

"Max?" Jeffrey's father asked. "Who's Max?"

Jeffrey wanted to clamp his hand over his mouth. But it was too late. The name had slipped out: *Max*. It was a name that Jeffrey could say in front of his friends, but not in front of his father. That was because Jeffrey's best friends—Ben, Ricky, Kenny, and Melissa—all knew about Max. They knew he was a cool guy who was a lot of fun to be with. They knew he made up wild and funny stories just like Jeffrey did. And they knew that he was totally different from all of the other fourth-graders. After all, how many fourth-graders at Redwood Elementary School had been born in the 1950s? Only one. And how many fourth-graders were ghosts? Only one. The one and only Max!

Mr. Becker stopped searching through a carton and frowned. "So who's Max? I've never heard you talk about him."

"Uh, well," Jeffrey said, thinking quickly. "Max is what we're calling Arvin Pubbler these days."

"What's wrong with Arvin?"

"Plenty, Dad," answered Jeffrey.

"I mean, what's wrong with Arvin's *name*?"

"Uh, well, we're trying to improve Arvin's

3

image. We figured that if we called him something else, we'd totally forget what a wimpo loser he is."

Mr. Becker shook his head and went back to looking for the baseball cards. In one corner of the attic was a stack of boxes he'd already opened. Just as Jeffrey finished his story about Arvin, the stack of boxes began to wobble and sway. Both Jeffrey and his father looked up. But only Jeffrey could see what was making the stack wobble.

It was Max. The ghost was sitting on top of the boxes, slowly coming into sight. Jeffrey grinned. He was glad to see Max—and he was just as glad that his dad *couldn't* see or hear him. It was great having a ghost for a secret, invisible friend.

Max wasn't like the ghosts in movies or books. Max was a boy about Jeffrey's age. He wore 1950s clothes: baggy blue jeans rolled at the cuffs and long-sleeved flannel plaid shirts buttoned at the collar. He liked baseball and rock 'n' roll and talking hip. The only problem was that what sounded hip to Max seemed like ancient history to Jeffrey. For example, Max's idea of rock 'n' roll was an old Elvis record.

"Hey, what's shaking, Daddy-o?" Max said to Jeffrey.

"You are," Jeffrey said, then stopped himself. He couldn't talk to Max now—not with his dad listening!

"I am what?" Mr. Becker asked. "And, Jeffrey, why are those boxes moving?"

"Uh, that must be where you packed all of the old salt *shakers*," Jeffrey answered. "Get it, Dad?" Then he looked over at the ghost. "We're looking for baseball cards," Jeffrey told Max.

"I haven't forgotten," answered Mr. Becker, because he thought Jeffrey was talking to him.

"Baseball cards? What a gas!" said the ghost. "Like, yours truly is the proud owner of at least a hundred baseball cards."

"I'm going to have *two* hundred cards when we find Dad's collection," Jeffrey said, to make the ghost jealous.

Mr. Becker gave his son a puzzled look.

Max shook his head. "Daddy-o, like, what I meant was, I always had a hundred cards *with* me. Back in my room I had at least one hundred *thousand* cards!" Like Jeffrey, Max liked to exaggerate.

"Yeah, I really believe it," Jeffrey said, smiling at his friend.

"You really believe what?" asked Mr. Becker.

"Uh, nothing, Dad," Jeffrey said quickly.

"Hey!" Mr. Becker bent over an open carton and pulled something out. "Well, what do you call this?"

Jeffrey looked at it. "I call it a shoe box," he said. "So far you've shown me five sweaters, two yearbooks, a box of baby clothes, and a scrapbook of canceled stamps. Please, Dad, I'm begging you. *Don't* show me your first pair of high-tops."

But Mr. Becker opened the shoe box, anyway. And then he motioned with his finger for Jeffrey to come and look.

There they were, inside the shoe box. His father's old baseball cards! They were in small stacks, each one wrapped with a red rubber band. Carefully, Mr. Becker picked up a pack, slid off the rubber band, and handed the cards to Jeffrey.

"Totally cool!" Jeffrey exclaimed, staring at the cards. They were players he had never seen in person or on TV. And they had weird haircuts and uniforms that were kind of baggy.

6

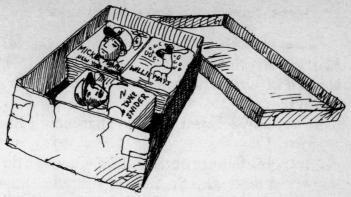

But Jeffrey knew the players' names right away. Mickey Mantle. Willie Mays. Duke Snider. They were all famous Hall of Fame players.

"Can I have them, Dad?" Jeffrey asked.

Mr. Becker shook his head. "I don't think I'm ready to give them up," he said. He began to flip through the cards. "Look at these," he said, more to himself than to Jeffrey. "I'd forgotten about some of these guys."

Max flew over to them and hovered over Jeffrey's shoulder.

"No, no, no, Daddy-o. You don't want these cards," Max told Jeffrey. "Like, every kid I know has them. Wait till you see my cards. I have triples of all those cool cats."

"But no one has cards like these anymore. They're super-old," Jeffrey said to Max, even though his father was listening.

"I know, Jeffrey," said Mr. Becker before Max could answer. "Tell you what. How about if I let you borrow the cards for a couple of days?"

Jeffrey's eyes went wide. "That would be so great! I'll—"

"But," his father continued, "I want you to be very careful with them." He smiled at Jeffrey and handed him the shoe box. "Show them to your friends, but don't lose them."

"No problem, Dad, sir!" Jeffrey said, giving his father a small but sincere salute. Then Jeffrey gave Max a "so there" smile. But Max had disappeared.

At school the next day, Jeffrey and his friends sat together in the cafeteria looking at baseball cards. They had spread them out all over the table so that there was hardly any room for their food. Jeffrey hadn't brought out his father's cards yet. He was saving them for a surprise.

"I've still got the most," Ricky Reyes said, eyeing everyone else's cards.

Ben shook his head. "It's not quantity but quality that counts."

"I totally agree," Melissa said, chomping on

8

a cherry tomato. "Face it, Ricky. You've got triples of Skippy Lendler, and I wouldn't take a Skippy Lendler card if you paid me."

"What's wrong with Skippy Lendler?" Ricky said. "I think he's cool."

"He's got the IQ of a jellyfish," Melissa answered.

"Hey," Ben protested, "that's an insult to all of the jellyfish in the world."

"Ha, ha," said Ricky.

"Admit it, Reyes," said Jeffrey. "Skippy Lendler probably doesn't know how to get from first base to second base."

"He doesn't have to know how," Melissa said with a giggle. "He never hits the ball hard enough to get a double."

Everyone laughed, including Ricky. Last year, if someone had made a joke like that, Ricky probably would have started a fight. Ricky was tough and he was on his way to becoming a karate expert, so he never took any smart-mouthing from anyone. But they were all fourth-graders now, and, more important, they were all friends.

"Okay, are you guys ready for my surprise?" Jeffrey asked. "My dad gave me *his* baseball cards. All oldies!"

"Wow!" Kenny Thompsen said. "He finally did? Let's see them!"

Jeffrey turned to reach into his backpack, which was hanging on the back of his chair. Before he could get the cards out, Arvin Pubbler walked up. Arvin was pudgy and whiny, and he always seemed to show up at the wrong time. "Hi, guys," he said. He was holding a tray full of food and eyeing the empty seat next to Kenny. "Cool baseball cards. Can I sit there?"

"No way, Arvin," Ricky Reyes told him.

"Why not?" Arvin whined.

"Because we're busy," Ricky said.

Jeffrey saw the hurt look on Arvin's face and decided to do something nice . . . sort of.

"Ricky means you *could* sit there," Jeffrey told Arvin, "but you really ought to go sit with Jenny Arthur instead. I think she likes you."

"Come on, Jeffrey," Arvin said with a little snort. "That's not true."

"Didn't she say she wanted to know where you were at all times?"

"Sure," said Arvin, "but that's so she can avoid me. She says I always step on her feet and get mud on her shoes."

"I think she wants to apologize, Arvin," Jef-

frey insisted. "Look, she's watching you right
now."

Arvin walked away and headed toward the
table where Jenny Arthur sat eating her trail
mix.

"Okay, he's gone," Ben said. "Come on, Jeffrey. Let's see your father's baseball cards."

"Yeah," said Melissa.

Jeffrey turned again to reach into his backpack.

Suddenly, from the other side of the room, there was a loud crash of dishes and the *plop* of food. Then everyone heard Jenny Arthur scream, "Arvin, you creep! You just spilled your whole tray of food on my shoes!"

Ricky started laughing right away. Ben, Kenny, and Melissa joined in. But Jeffrey didn't laugh. In fact, he started to sweat. His hands were searching every inch of his backpack. "Oh, no," he said over and over.

"Jeffrey, what's wrong?" asked Melissa.

"The cards," he said in a panic. "My dad's baseball cards. They're gone!"

Chapter Two

"This isn't happening," Jeffrey moaned. He couldn't believe that his father's baseball cards were gone from his backpack. It was the worst possible thing that could have happened. He had promised not to lose them!

Jeffrey stood and shook the backpack so that everything inside tumbled onto the cafeteria table. There were two comic books, a week's supply of rainbow-fruit bubble gum, and a small puddle of fake, rubber blood. Finally, Jeffrey's lunch fell out of the backpack, along with a sheet of homework that Jeffrey had not filled out.

"That's ancient history," Ben said, looking at the homework.

"Uh-uh," Kenny said. "It's math. Looks like Jeffrey never turned it in."

"No. It's ancient history," Ben repeated with authority. "It was due last year!"

"Who cares?" Jeffrey asked, turning his backpack inside out to make certain it was empty. "Where are my dad's baseball cards? Someone took them!"

Jeffrey's friends watched with worried

looks on their faces as Jeffrey sat down. He slumped with his elbows bent and his head in his hands. "I can't believe I lost his cards. I'm in major trouble."

"Your dad's going to kill you, huh?" said Kenny.

"Worse," Jeffrey answered. "He'll just say the four most horrible words in the world. He'll say: 'I'm disappointed in you.'"

Ricky nodded. "That's definitely the worst. I can't stand it when my dad says that to me."

"What are you going to do, Jeffrey?" asked Melissa.

"I don't know. But the next time you see me, I might be on the side of a milk carton," Jeffrey said glumly.

"Oh, Daddy-o. Don't talk about running away," a voice said suddenly.

Jeffrey looked up, and there was Max, slowly coming into view. "Max!" he called out.

The ghost hovered in the air next to Jeffrey. He smiled at everyone at the table. "Hey, buddy-os," Max said, greeting Jeffrey and his friends. "Cheer up. I've got something for you to lay your eyeballs on. And you cats better get your shovels ready so that you can dig it the most."

"Dig it?" said Kenny. "You mean we're going outside?"

"No, that's a 1950s expression," Jeffrey explained. "It means we're going to like it."

"What is it, Max?" Melissa asked.

"Oh, nothing," teased the ghost. "Just the best baseball cards known to man." And with that he took out five stacks of old baseball cards wrapped with red rubber bands.

"Max! Those are my dad's baseball cards!" Jeffrey said. He didn't know what emotion to feel first: happy, surprised, angry, or relieved. "Max! You took them out of my backpack?"

"Daddy-o, I did not *take* your cards," said the ghost, sounding a bit hurt. He shook his head at Jeffrey. "Like, sometimes I *take* my time or *take* my temperature or *take* a bus. But I wouldn't *take* your old man's cards. Like, I just borrowed them, that's all."

Jeffrey held out his hand. He wanted Max to give him his dad's baseball cards back. But instead the ghost slapped Jeffrey's hand in a friendly way.

"Daddy-o, I'm glad you're not mad at me," Max said. "Now, let me show everyone these cards. They aren't as hip as mine, of course, but they're cool."

15

Jeffrey knew there was nothing he could do to stop the ghost. When Max got an idea into his head, he went through with it, no matter what Jeffrey did.

So Jeffrey just sat back and watched while Max showed everyone Mr. Becker's baseball cards.

"This cat's name is Mickey Mantle," said Max, laying down one of the old cards. "But he's just from rookiesville. He probably won't last more than a year in the big league. You'd better throw this card away, Jeffrey."

Jeffrey rolled his eyes. "Max, Mickey Mantle became one of the best hitters ever. And all of these cards are worth big bucks. They're really old."

"Old? I bought some just like these a few weeks ago . . . right before I took my one-way trip to ghostsville," Max said.

"But that was in the 1950s," said Ben.

Max looked confused.

Ricky picked up the Mickey Mantle card. "Is your dad going to let you keep all of these?" he asked.

Jeffrey shook his head. "I gotta give them right back."

"It's an awesome collection, Jeffrey. Totally radical," Melissa announced.

"Thanks." Jeffrey couldn't stop smiling. Even if the cards weren't his to keep, he knew how cool it was to be able to show them around.

Just then a voice called to Jeffrey and his friends: "Hey, geeks!"

Without even looking up, Jeffrey knew who it was. It was Brian Carr, the most obnoxious kid in the fourth grade. Brian was even worse than Arvin Pubbler because Brian liked to start fights and break things. Arvin was just a whiner and a wimp.

Max hated Brian just as much as Jeffrey did, and the instant he heard Brian's voice he disappeared. But before he vanished, he handed Jeffrey's baseball cards to Kenny.

"What's up?" Brian asked. He leaned toward the table between Kenny and Melissa. They moved away from him as if bugs were jumping off him.

"Go away, Brian," Ben said.

Brian, of course, ignored him. "Hey, what's that?" he said, staring at the cards Kenny was holding.

17

Before Jeffrey could stop him, Brian made a grab for the first stack of cards. And Kenny was too nice and too shy to resist. Jeffrey watched in horror as his father's baseball cards quickly changed from Kenny's hands to Brian's.

"Hey, give those back," Jeffrey said.

"I'm just looking," Brian said. He flipped through Jeffrey's dad's cards roughly.

"Can't you look without bending them in half?" Jeffrey snapped, reaching for them.

But Brian pulled the cards close to his chest and moved back. "I'll buy them from you. How much?"

"They aren't for sale," Jeffrey said.

"Good." Brian put the cards in his shirt pocket. "Then I'll just keep them."

Jeffrey's heart began to pound. "They're my dad's," he explained, trying to sound calm. "They don't belong to me."

Brian took the cards out of his pocket and stared at them. Then he stared at Jeffrey. Finally he reached across the table, grabbing at Jeffrey's shirt. But Jeffrey leaned back and Brian missed. A minute later an important-sounding voice interrupted everything with an important-sounding announcement over the school's P.A. system.

18

"Brian Carr, will you please make the scene at the principal's office?" said the voice. "Like, the president of the United States is here to see you. And he is strictly from hurry-upsville."

Brian froze. "The president is here to see me?" he mumbled. "What does he want? What should I say?"

Jeffrey couldn't answer. He was trying too hard to keep a straight face.

Ricky Reyes took over. First, he removed the cards from Brian's hand and gave them to Jeffrey. "Whatever you say, keep it simple, Carr," he told him. "You don't know too many words."

Jeffrey and his friends tried to smother their laughter as Brian went rushing toward the principal's office.

"I can't believe that," Melissa said when Brian had gone. "How did Max get to the principal's office fast enough to make that announcement?"

"If there's one thing Max knows, it's the fastest way to the principal's office," Jeffrey answered with a laugh.

"No muss, no fuss, no sweat, Daddy-os."

Jeffrey looked around to see where Max's

voice was coming from now. "Max?" he called softly.

"The one and only," Max said as he materialized so that everyone could see him.

"How'd you get back here so fast?" Kenny asked in amazement.

"I *flew*," Max said with a grin. "Did you dig my announcement on the P.A. system?"

"Totally," Jeffrey and Melissa both said at once.

"Good," said the ghost. "Then you can pay me back by letting me spend some more old timesville with your old man's baseball cards."

"No way," Jeffrey started to say. But he was too late. The ghost had already swooped down and picked up the cards. "Daddy-o, daddy-o, don't get maddy-o. Like, leave them alone and they'll come home. Your baseball cards will be in your desk right after lunch."

"But lunch is over now," Jeffrey told him.

"Okay, then right after music class," Max said.

"Do you promise?" asked Jeffrey, knowing that the ghost wasn't exactly reliable.

Max made himself look very innocent. "My word is my promise."

"I'd feel better if you really promised," Jeffrey said. "Do you?"

"See you later, alligator." Max gave everyone a big wave before he disappeared completely.

"I don't think he answered you," said Melissa.

"I know." Jeffrey sighed. "He never does."

Jeffrey worried about his father's baseball cards all through music class. Today they were singing songs about Spain, and it felt as if the class would go on forever. They had sung about sombreros, and now they were singing about the rain, and Jeffrey knew he couldn't wait any longer. He decided he had to do something to get out of music class early.

"Ms. Voss," he said, raising his hand. The music teacher looked up from the piano. "You know what would be fun? If we sang all the songs today twice as fast."

"Oh, Jeffrey," Ms. Voss said with a laugh. "If we did that, class would be over in half the time. And we wouldn't want to miss out on half the fun, would we?"

Ms. Voss, the music teacher, was the second oldest teacher in the school—next to Jeffrey's regular teacher, Miss Dotson. Ms. Voss had a sweet, happy personality and a musical voice—even when she wasn't singing.

"But, Ms. Voss," Jeffrey went on, "next week we could sing everything twice as slow and then we'd be all caught up."

Ms. Voss shook her head and went on singing about the rain in Spain. Jeffrey knew he had to try something else.

"Ms. Voss," he said, not even raising his hand. "Don't you think I'm being totally disruptive? Maybe you should send me back to my classroom."

But Ms. Voss just kept singing, and the class sang with her. Jeffrey was stuck.

Halfway through the song, however, Ms. Voss stopped playing. "Arvin Pubbler," she said, "did you know you were singing off-key?"

"I wasn't singing," Arvin replied, rocking in his seat and holding his stomach. "I was moaning. Ms. Voss, I have to go see the nurse. Right away. Can I, huh? Can I?"

"Arvin, you ask to go to the nurse's office every week," said Ms. Voss.

"I can't help it," Arvin whined. "I have a stomach ache."

Ms. Voss shook her head. "All right, Arvin. Go to the nurse."

"Thanks, Ms. Voss," Arvin said, moaning all the way to the door.

Jeffrey watched Arvin leave and wondered if he should have a stomach ache, too. Then he could go back to his classroom and wait for Max to show up with his dad's baseball cards. But he knew Ms. Voss wouldn't fall for it. She thought everything Jeffrey said was a joke.

Jeffrey had to sit through five more songs about Spain before music class was finally over. Then he hurried back to his classroom and started looking in his desk.

"Class, take out paper and pencil," he heard his teacher, Miss Dotson, say. "I'm going to give you a surprise science quiz."

A surprise science quiz? Jeffrey didn't even care. All he cared about were the baseball cards that Max had not quite promised to return.

He reached into his desk and felt around way in the back. Then he bent his head down and looked inside. He checked every corner, but the cards weren't there. Max had let him down again!

Chapter Three

Jeffrey took one more look inside his desk and then sat down with a moan. Everyone in the class was getting ready for Miss Dotson's quiz.

"Jeffrey, what's wrong with you?" Melissa asked. She leaned across her desk, which was right next to Jeffrey's, and poked him in the side with her pencil. "You look weird."

"Max didn't show up," Jeffrey said. "He promised to leave my dad's baseball cards right in my desk after music class, but they aren't here."

"Relax," Melissa said. "Max is probably just late. You know Max."

Right! Max was late, that's all. That sounded a lot better than Max completely forgot, or Max accidentally dropped them in a puddle, or Max used them to line the bottom of the rabbit's cage in the science room. Jeffrey relaxed, but not for long.

For the next half hour Jeffrey worked on the surprise science quiz. He knew most of the answers, but it was hard to remember them when all he could think about was the baseball cards.

Next Miss Dotson announced that she wanted everyone in the class to write a one-page story. The subject was: What would happen if cats could talk. Jeffrey couldn't help it; in his story, a cat named Mickey talked about baseball cards.

Finally the bell rang. School was over and Max still hadn't returned the baseball cards. Jeffrey and his friends went looking for the ghost in the park across from the school. That was their usual meeting place on the days when Max cut class, which was most of the time.

"Yo, Max!" Jeffrey called, looking around.

Instantly the ghost appeared, smiling and sitting in a large pine tree.

"Max, where are my dad's baseball cards?" Jeffrey called up to his friend. "Why didn't you bring them back? You practically promised."

The ghost ran a hand through his slicked-back hair. "I promised and I delivered, Daddy-o. I gave them back."

"No, you didn't," Jeffrey argued. "I looked inside my desk. They weren't in there."

"That's because I laid them *on* your desk," answered the ghost.

Jeffrey started walking in circles. "*On* my desk? I said put them *in* my desk!"

"On . . . in . . . like, what's the big dif, Daddy-o? I only blew it by one letter."

"Max, why don't you ever do anything I ask you to do? My dad's really going to be mad at me."

"Like, sorry," Max said seriously. "How about if I give you *my* set of baseball cards? Your old daddy-o will never know the difference."

"Oh, yes, he will," Jeffrey moaned. "He's

memorized every wrinkle and crease in those cards."

"Wait a minute, Jeffrey," Melissa said. "You're missing the point." She was wearing her football-huddle face—serious and totally focused on the next play. "Max put the cards *on* your desk. Right, Max?"

"Like, if you were any more right you'd be left," the ghost said quickly.

"But," continued Melissa, "the cards weren't there when you got back to class, right, Jeffrey?"

Jeffrey nodded.

"So what happened to them?" asked Ben.

There was only one answer, but it was too awful to be true. "Someone took them," Jeffrey said.

"You mean thievesville?" Max asked.

Melissa's eyes were angry. "And there's only one person who's fast enough and mean enough and thinks he's smart enough to do something like this," she concluded. "Brian Carr."

"Yeah, he was really after those baseball cards in the cafeteria today," Ricky Reyes agreed.

"Well, what are we waiting for?" said Max.

27

"Like, let's pretend Brian Carr's a big front lawn and go rake his leaves!"

"Not so fast, you guys," said Ben. He waited until everyone was listening to him. "Brian Carr's not our only suspect. Just when we were coming back from music class, I saw Melissa's older brother, Gary. He was walking out of our classroom. I thought that was strange."

"What's strange about it is that he was walking and not oozing under the door like the slimeball he is," Melissa said.

"Do you think Gary would really sneak into our classroom and steal Jeffrey's cards?" asked Kenny. Kenny always waited until the last possible moment before believing that someone was a rat.

"Let me put it this way," Melissa explained. "Gary's favorite hobby is taking collars off lost dogs so that they can't be returned to their owners."

"Whew." Ricky whistled. "Prime-time bad."

"Gary or Brian? Like, come on, Daddy-os. Who is it?"

Jeffrey shrugged. It was a real mystery.

Then Kenny spoke up. "Maybe neither," he

said. Everyone stared at him for an explanation, and he blushed. "How about Miss Dotson?" he asked quietly.

"Miss Dotson?" everyone repeated.

"Well, you know she's always forgetting things and losing things," Kenny told them. "Maybe she took your baseball cards and forgot to tell you, Jeffrey."

"It's possible," Melissa said. "Just like she took my diary in September and forgot to give it back."

Two suspects were confusing enough. But three was almost unfair. "We've got to start thinking like detectives," Jeffrey announced.

"Right. We've got to find some clues," Ben said. "Let's start at the scene of the crime. Miss Dotson's classroom."

"But how can we get in?" Kenny asked. "The school's probably locked up by now."

"Daddy-o," Max said, putting a brotherly arm around Kenny's shoulder, "like, ghosts laugh at locked doors."

So Max led the way back to the school building. Then he walked right up to the front door—and went right through it! He opened the door from the inside and motioned for the others to come in.

Ricky, Melissa, and Kenny said they would stay outside as guards. So Jeffrey and Ben tiptoed into the school and across the squeaky tile floor toward Miss Dotson's classroom. Max walked on tiptoes, too. But he was floating two feet above the floor, so it really didn't matter.

"Max," whispered Jeffrey when they reached Miss Dotson's door. "Stay outside and give us a signal if you see anyone coming."

Then Jeffrey and Ben went into the empty classroom alone.

"What kind of clues are we looking for?" Jeffrey asked.

"I'm going to dust for fingerprints," Ben said.

"That's weird," Jeffrey said. "My mom always dusts the house to get rid of them."

"Ha, ha," Ben said. But he knew exactly what to do. He took two chalkboard erasers and clapped them together. The white chalk dust fell on Jeffrey's desk like snow. Then Ben leaned close and observed the desk with a keen scientist's eye.

"Do you see any fingerprints?" asked Jeffrey.

"Jelly prints, bubble-gum prints, and spit-ball prints," Ben said. "No fingerprints. Let's examine the contents of your desk."

Ben lifted the lid, but he dropped it again immediately. A terrible smell was coming from inside Jeffrey's desk. "Jeffrey, what's in there?"

"My mom gave me a tuna and liverwurst sandwich for lunch a couple of weeks ago. I haven't decided yet whether to eat it or not."

Ben frowned. "Give it another week and it may eat you."

Suddenly, the classroom door opened with a bang. It happened so fast that Jeffrey and Ben jumped straight up into the air.

Quickly, Max poked his head in the doorway. "Nobody's coming. The coast is clear," he announced.

Jeffrey allowed himself to start breathing again. "Max! You were only supposed to warn us if someone *was* coming."

"I'm hip, Daddy-o. But, like, that would be *bad* news. I thought you cats would dig hearing some *good* news. Like, everything's cool."

Ben shook his head. "Jeffrey, if you had to find a ghost in your desk last year, why couldn't it be a normal ghost who scared people by saying 'Boo!' "

"Let's just get out of here," Jeffrey said.

As soon as Ben, Jeffrey, and Max got outside, their friends had some news of their own.

"We saw Miss Dotson," Melissa said.

"I talked to her," Kenny said. "I asked her if she took some baseball cards off your desk. But she said no. She said you probably lost them, Jeffrey. Her advice is: 'Don't worry. You'll find them someday when you least expect it.' That's what always happens to her."

Jeffrey groaned. "I can't wait for someday. I've got to find them right now," he insisted. "And we didn't find any clues."

"Then it's back to square one," Max said.

"What do you mean?" Jeffrey asked the ghost.

"I mean the number-one square around here," Max said. "Brian Carr."

"Good idea," Melissa said. "He's our number-one suspect, anyway."

"And I know just where to find him," Ricky Reyes said.

Ricky Reyes led the way and everyone else followed. As they walked, he explained that

Brian did the same thing every day after school. "He's such a bully, he doesn't have any friends. So he goes over to his dad's bowling alley and hangs out there," Ricky explained.

When they got to the bowling alley, it was noisy and crowded. All but one of the twelve lanes were being used. The air was filled with the smack of bowling balls on the wood lanes and the crash of the pins falling. They also heard Mr. Carr, yelling at the top of his lungs, "Brian, will you get off that lane with your bicycle!"

"I groove on bowling the most," said Max. "I once scored four hundred points."

"The highest you can score officially is three hundred points, Max," said Ben.

Max gave Ben a scornful look. "I *was* the official," he said. "And it was officially cool to score the four big O's."

"Well, maybe you can do it again," Jeffrey suggested. "Why don't you go bowl a few lanes, Max?"

"Truly, Daddy-o? That would be coolsville with me," Max said. "See you later, bowling 'gators." And with that he floated off toward the one empty lane.

Jeffrey didn't mind getting rid of Max for a while. He wanted to deal with Brian Carr himself. Quickly, he scanned the bowling alley. There was a bunch of kids from school renting bowling shoes, but Brian was sitting in the snack area. He was stacking up french fries like a brick wall, using ketchup as the mortar. On the floor next to Brian was his red backpack.

"Guys, I think this case is just about wrapped up," Jeffrey said to his friends. "I'll bet my cards are in Brian's backpack right now."

"I've got an idea!" said Kenny, who was really getting into this detective business. "I'll walk over there and pretend to drop my backpack. Then I'll pick up a backpack and walk away with it. But it won't be mine. It'll be Brian's."

"That plan is ninety-percent there," Ben

34

said. "The only trouble is, Brian's bag is red and yours is green."

"It still might work," Kenny said. "If Brian's not looking."

"Or even if he is looking," Jeffrey chimed in. "I'm not sure Brian has learned all of his colors yet. But let me do it, Kenny. I want to handle this myself."

Jeffrey walked up behind Brian without being seen. Then he pretended to drop his backpack. He smiled to himself. It was working! Brian didn't even turn around! Now all he had to do was pick up Brian's bag and carry it away. He reached down. His fingers were almost touching the bag, almost closing around the back straps. Then, out of nowhere, a voice called out, "Hey, Jeffrey!" Suddenly, Arvin Pubbler rushed over and pushed Jeffrey's hand away.

"You almost picked up the wrong bag," Arvin said. "It's a good thing I was here. I just helped you out of one of life's embarrassing situations."

"How can I ever pay you back?" Jeffrey muttered.

At that moment Brian Carr turned around. "What are you trying to do with my backpack,

35

Becker?" he demanded. He grabbed his bag up off the floor.

"Why would I want your backpack, Brian?" Jeffrey asked. He watched Brian's face carefully for any clues. "You don't have anything of mine, do you?"

Brian didn't say yes and he didn't say no. He just laughed and said, "Arvin, go ask my dad for a cherry soda."

"I don't like cherry soda," Arvin protested.

"It's not for you, it's for me!" Brian said with a sneer.

Jeffrey could tell that he wasn't going to get Brian to give him any more information. He turned around and walked away—past his friends, out of the bowling alley, and straight for his house. There was nothing he could do about it. His dad's baseball cards were gone, and he didn't have a clue who had stolen them. So he was going to have to do something awful. Something horrible. Something he hadn't done in a long, long time. He was going to have to tell his father the truth!

Chapter Four

As Jeffrey walked home from the bowling alley, he tried to think of the best way to tell his dad the terrible news. His dad's collection of old baseball cards was gone. That was the truth. But he couldn't just blurt it out that way. Somehow, he had to find a way to soften the blow.

Maybe he could say something like: "Dad, it was awful. I was robbed on the way home. These three big kids surrounded me. Boy, were they big. Anyway, they said, 'Give us your cash or you're sidewalk mush!' But I thought they said, 'Give us your dad's baseball cards.' So I did. At least I'm still alive. That's what counts, isn't it?"

Jeffrey frowned. It was a great story. Hollywood could probably make a movie out of it. But he just couldn't do it to his dad. Still, he knew that telling the truth was the right thing to do. But the more he thought about it, the less he wanted to do it. If I go home and tell Dad I lost his cards, he'll be miserable, he reasoned. But if I find them first, he'll be happy. So which do I want him to be: miserable or happy?

When he looked at it that way, the choice was easy. And besides, Jeffrey thought, why should I give up so soon? There was a mystery to be solved! And he knew exactly how to investigate his next suspect.

So Jeffrey hung around in his backyard until Melissa, who lived next door, got home. Then he knocked at her back door. Mrs. McKane answered it.

"Hi, Mrs. McKane. May I stay for dinner?" asked Jeffrey in his friendliest voice.

"Well." Mrs. McKane sounded startled by his bold request. "We were just sitting down to eat . . . but all right. Come in. We have extras tonight, anyway."

"Thanks, Mrs. McKane," Jeffrey said. "I'd better call home and let my parents know." Luckily, it was Jeffrey's mother who answered the phone; she thought it was fine that he was eating at the McKanes'.

Jeffrey quickly took a seat at the dinner table next to Melissa. He spread his napkin on his lap. "Hi," he whispered to his friend.

"What's going on?" Melissa asked quietly while her mother brought the food to the table. "Where did you go after the bowling alley? We couldn't find you."

"I walked home and thought of a new plan. I'm here to spy on suspect number two—your big brother, Gary," he whispered back.

Melissa frowned and started to tell Jeffrey something. But just then her father came into the kitchen.

"Hi, Jeffrey," said Mr. McKane. "What are you doing here? Did your mother make asparagus casserole again?"

"No, I came over because . . . uh, well . . . because my mom is going to have a baby," Jeffrey explained. "I've got to learn everything I can about being an older brother. So I came over to observe how Gary acts around Melissa."

"Well, you're out of luck, Jeffrey," said Mr. McKane, bringing bowls of salad from the counter. "Gary's not here."

"That's what I was trying to tell you," Melissa said. "He's staying at his friend Michael Block's house tonight."

"Oh," Jeffrey said, leaning way back in his chair.

"He said something about . . . now what was it?" Mrs. McKane asked herself, stopping as

she poured glasses of milk. "Oh, yes. He said he wanted to show Michael his new set of baseball cards."

Crash! Jeffrey's chair fell over backward onto the kitchen floor.

"Jeffrey, are you all right?" asked Mr. McKane.

"Uh, sure," Jeffrey said, getting up. "Did you say *new* baseball cards, Mrs. McKane?"

Mrs. McKane nodded. "They're old ones, I think, but he just got them today, so they're new."

New old baseball cards? It was all beginning to make sense to Jeffrey. Gary was the thief—and Jeffrey was going to catch him red-handed! But first he had to get out of eating dinner at Melissa's house.

"Uh, Mrs. McKane," Jeffrey said. "Now I remember why I really came over. My mom wants Melissa to come eat at my house."

"What?" said both of Melissa's parents at once.

"Well, just in case the new baby is a girl, Mom wants me to see how a girl eats. Okay?"

But Melissa wouldn't budge. "I'm not going anywhere, Jeffrey. My mom made everything I like for dinner since Gary's not home."

"We've got to go to Michael Block's house to spy on Gary," Jeffrey whispered.

"*After* dinner," Melissa said, stomping her foot.

Jeffrey ate dinner quickly. He hardly tasted his food. He was too busy thinking about all of the rotten things Gary had done to him, to Melissa, and to their friends over the years. Stealing his dad's baseball cards was just about the worst. Jeffrey wanted revenge, and he wanted it bad.

But Melissa took her time eating, enjoying every bite.

41

As soon as dinner was over, Jeffrey and Melissa left to go to Michael Block's house. But first Jeffrey made a quick stop at a corner carry-out. He bought a bag full of jelly-and-cream-filled Ring-A-Loop cakes.

"How can you still be hungry after my mom's dinner?" Melissa asked on their way to the Blocks' house. "I'm stuffed."

"You'll see," Jeffrey answered with a smile. "It's all part of my plan to catch Gary with my baseball cards."

"You don't know for sure that he took them."

"But the clues all add up, Melissa. Ben said he saw Gary coming out of our classroom today, and now your mom says he has new old baseball cards. Gary's our rat, and we've got him trapped."

Michael Block's house was a two-story wooden house. It was only four blocks away from the McKanes', so it didn't take them long to get there. The Blocks' front yard was separated from the sidewalk and the street by a high wire fence. It had to be high because on the other side of it was Bootsie, Michael Block's dog. Everyone in the neighborhood knew that there were three important things that Bootsie had never learned. She had never learned when to stop growing. She had never learned when to stop barking. And apparently she had never ever been told that a dog was supposed to be a person's best friend. She hated everyone and everything that moved.

Bootsie started growling the instant Jeffrey and Melissa walked up in front of the fence.

"There's Gary and Michael," Melissa said.

She was pointing up toward a window on the second floor where the lights were turned up bright and the rock 'n' roll music was turned up loud. Every now and then Michael or Gary would move past the window playing an air guitar. "The perfect instrument for a couple of airheads," Melissa said, laughing.

Maybe it was Melissa's laugh. Or maybe it was the fact that she pointed at the house. But something set Bootsie off like a burglar alarm. The dog started barking and barking and barking. And while she was barking, she was also jumping and jumping and jumping with all her strength against the wire-mesh fence. She was trying to get at Melissa and Jeffrey.

Jeffrey looked past the dog at a tall tree with lots of thick, armlike branches. It looked like a great tree to climb. But better than that, it

43

stood right in front of Michael Block's room.

"If we could climb that tree, we could see into Michael's window. And then we'd see if Gary's got my dad's cards," Jeffrey said.

"Great," Melissa said. "But how are we going to get past this barking maniac?"

That's when Jeffrey took out the bag of Ring-A-Loop cakes. He shook it in Bootsie's face.

The dog's barking instantly became a whimper. Bootsie had a weakness for sweet treats, and Jeffrey knew it. When Jeffrey started tossing the cakes as far as he could all over the yard, the dog went after every one.

While Bootsie chewed on the goodies, Jeffrey and Melissa made a run for the tall tree in the front yard.

"Follow me," Melissa said, scrambling up first. She climbed hand over hand, higher and higher, to where the branches became thinner. When she was about twenty feet from the ground, she wrapped her arms and legs around a branch. Then she scooted away from the tree trunk and toward the end of the limb.

Melissa was a fearless climber, and it took Jeffrey a little longer to join her on the branch. But when he did, the two of them had front-row seats. They were two stories off the ground and just a few feet away from Michael Block's bedroom window.

Through it Melissa and Jeffrey could see the two sixth-graders. They were sitting on the floor of Michael's room laughing and pushing each other. And they were passing baseball cards back and forth!

Jeffrey was trying his hardest to squint to see the cards more clearly. But he was just a little too far away to tell. "If they'd open the window, I bet I could see if they're mine."

"Hey, what's that?" Melissa asked. "Something's blocking our view."

Jeffrey saw it, too. It was like a dark cloud that suddenly dropped down from the sky and settled in front of the bedroom window.

"Look!" Jeffrey said.

The cloud started to disappear, and a minute later they saw Max! For once he wasn't wearing blue jeans and a plaid flannel shirt. He was wearing a long raincoat that drooped below his feet—although, since he was floating in midair, it didn't drag on the ground. He was also wearing a hat with a wide brim, just like a detective from the 1940s and 1950s. And he was holding a large magnifying glass up to

45

his face. The round spyglass was about as big as Max's head.

"Max! What are you doing here?" Jeffrey hissed.

"Digging the clue scene, Daddy-o. I'm cool on the trail," the ghost said in his most mysterious voice. Then he floated gently to the tree to join his friends.

"Don't you mean *hot* on the trail?" asked Melissa.

Max shook his head. "No. Everything I do is cool. But why are you cats making this scene? Did you climb that tree or did you sit on an acorn twenty years ago?"

"We're trying to see what Gary and Michael are doing in there," Jeffrey explained.

"Daddy-o, they're digging some baseball cards. And they look like good ones—although not as cool as mine."

"I'll bet they're my dad's cards," Jeffrey said. "I wish I could see them."

Max floated back toward the house. "That's as easy as one-two," said the ghost. "Just leave it to me."

"Don't you mean one-two-three, Max?" asked Melissa.

"Nope. When I'm through with them, these

46

cats will be running so fast, they won't have time to count to three. Watch this, Daddy-os." Max floated up to the window. And then he floated right through the window—and into Michael Block's bedroom!

How was Max going to scare them? Jeffrey wondered. Was he going to make the lights flash? Was he going to throw things around the room? Jeffrey and Melissa waited and watched.

At first Gary and Michael didn't notice a thing. They didn't notice that a ghost was sitting down on Michael's bed. And they didn't notice that the top sheet began to move. But when Max pulled the sheet over his head and then started flying around the room, Gary and Michael really noticed!

Even with the window closed, Melissa and Jeffrey could hear them screaming as they jumped to their feet. They started running around the room, climbing over the bed and practically knocking each other down as they tried to get out the door.

As soon as they were gone, Max opened the bedroom window. "The coast is clearsville," he said.

Jeffrey stood up on the branch. It was a thick one that reached right to Michael's window. Still, it was a long way down if he fell. Bravely, he inched his way to the windowsill, and Max pulled him in. Melissa scrambled in without any help at all.

Jeffrey didn't waste a minute. There were baseball cards all over the room, scattered everywhere. Gary had thrown them all over the place when Max scared them to death. So Jeffrey immediately started going around and picking them up, checking to see if they were his father's cards.

"Well?" Max asked, sounding very proud of

himself. "Like, are these your old man's cards or not?"

Finally, Jeffrey looked over at Max and said, "No. They're different. And it's a good thing, too, because look. Gary scribbled all over these cards."

Max looked at the baseball cards Jeffrey held out to him. On each player's face Gary had drawn a mustache or a beard or a zigzag scar with a ballpoint pen. It was a typical Gary kind of joke—not funny at all but totally destructive.

"Gary's a certified slimeball," Melissa said.

"But he's not the slimeball who stole my cards," Jeffrey added. "And now I've got to go home empty-handed."

When Jeffrey got home that night, his father was lying on the couch. He was reading a mystery novel and trying to guess the ending.

I wish I knew the ending to the case of the missing baseball cards, Jeffrey thought.

"Hey, Jeffrey, did your friends like my baseball cards?" asked Mr. Becker when he heard Jeffrey come in.

"Like them?" Jeffrey said. "They couldn't keep their hands off them."

"Great," said his father. "Leave them on my desk. I'll put them away later."

"Well, Dad, I'm not really ready to give them back to you," Jeffrey said nervously.

"Why not?" Mr. Becker asked in a serious voice.

"Dad, I don't have them. I mean, here's what really happened. I put them in my backpack. And then I put my backpack on before I left school. But it was really, uh, Brian Carr's backpack. And he took mine. So your cards are in Brian's backpack."

"That means all you have to do is call Brian up to get your backpack and my cards," said Mr. Becker.

"Right!" Jeffrey said. "But the only problem is, I think Brian is out of town. His Boy Scout troop is on a secret mission for the CIA."

Mr. Becker shook his head. "How about if I give you until Monday to get my cards back?"

"Monday? Sure. No problem, Dad. Two days? Monday? Yeah. Great. Just one thing, Dad." Jeffrey had to ask. "Do you mean *this* Monday?"

Chapter Five

With only two days left to find his dad's baseball cards, Jeffrey was in a panic. And the two days weren't even school days! They were weekend days: Saturday and Sunday. How was he supposed to catch a school thief when he wasn't even in school?

Luckily, Saturday *was* a school day—sort of. It was the day of the annual Redwood Elementary School Fall Festival. The Fall Festival was a cross between a carnival, a flea market, and a fair. There were games, food, prizes, a junk sale, a raffle, and all kinds of other special activities set up in colorful booths on the playground. The parents and teachers had decorated the whole area with balloons and the banners that each class had made.

Jeffrey, Ben, Kenny, and Ricky all walked to the Fall Festival together and talked about the mystery at hand.

"This is my last chance," Jeffrey said. "I've got to get my dad's cards back today—or else."

"Where's Melissa?" Ben asked.

"She went with Becky Singer," Jeffrey replied.

"Okay, so it's just us. We're on our own," Ben announced. Then he proceeded to give Ricky and Kenny an outline of his plan—his plan to solve the case of the missing baseball cards! Ben had worked it out with Jeffrey on the phone the night before. "It's like this," Ben began, taking a sip from the can of soda he was carrying. "The sixth-graders are having a baseball-card trading and selling booth."

"How do you know?" Ricky asked, surprised.

"My mom's best friend is helping to set it up," Ben explained. "It works like this: For fifty cents you can set up your whole collection of cards and sell off the best ones. Or you can just hang around there and trade with other kids—even kids you don't know. So we're going to take turns hanging around there all day. That way, I'm hoping, we'll catch the thief."

"How?" Kenny wanted to know.

"We'll stake out the booth," Jeffrey said, taking over the explanation. "Ben has a theory that whoever stole my cards will show up there."

"You could be right," Kenny agreed. "The thief will probably want to show off your dad's old cards and stuff."

"Right," Ben said. "So we're going to take turns hanging around."

"And we'll act like we want to make some big trades, like five cards for one. But only for certain cards."

"Which just happen to be the same as the cards Jeffrey lost," Ben said. "As soon as that guy tries to trade one of Jeffrey's dad's cards, we've got him." Ben took another sip from his can of soda. "Besides that, we may even get a picture of the guy."

"We will? How?" asked Jeffrey.

It was then that Ben unveiled his latest invention. He opened up the back of his soda can and turned it around so that everyone could see.

"Wow! There's a little camera in there," Kenny said.

"Yep. It's my dad's. I've been testing it out, taking pictures of you guys the whole time we've been walking," Ben said. "Whoever is on duty in the trading booth will have the camera. We'll take pictures of anyone who looks suspicious."

Jeffrey gave Ben a relieved smile. With a friend like him, how could he lose? He'd catch the thief for sure. In fact, he felt so confident, he decided to relax and have a really good time at the Fall Festival.

Ricky took the first shift watching the action at the baseball-card booth, and Ben gave him his soda-can hidden camera. Kenny went to work at the Guess Your Weight booth, which he had promised Miss Dotson he would do. That left Jeffrey and Ben to go around together exploring the rest of the festival booths.

First thing, they went straight to the fortune-teller's booth to see if they were going to have good luck at catching the thief.

The fortune-teller was inside a small camping tent. There was a sign on the flap that said MADAME ESMERELDA KNOWS ALL, SEES ALL, AND HAS A BIG MOUTH!

Jeffrey and Ben entered the tent. It was dimly lit by two flickering candles. A woman dressed in colorful clothes with lots of bright scarves tied around her sat on a folding chair. In front of her was a small round table with a crystal ball on top.

"I am Madame Esmerelda," she said in a funny, made-up voice.

54

"Gee, she looks just like Jenny Arthur's mother," Jeffrey said to Ben.

But Madame Esmerelda interrupted him. "Not today, bub. Do you dare to know what the future holds in store for you?"

"Not me," said Ben. "Fortune-telling has been proven to be totally unscientific. Besides, I'm not lucky at these things."

"I predicted that you were going to say those very words," said Madame Esmerelda. "See, I do know everything."

Jeffrey handed the fortune-teller one of his tickets, then sat down in the chair.

"Let me see your palm," she said, pointing to his right hand with one of her long purple fingernails.

"Am I going to have good luck today?" Jeffrey asked.

The woman traced the lines on Jeffrey's palm with her finger. "Well, I see you have a very long lunch line. That means you're used to waiting for things. And you see how this line ends with a hook? That's your fishing line. Are you trying to catch something today?"

Jeffrey looked quickly at Ben. "Yes," Jeffrey said excitedly. "How did you know?"

Madame Esmerelda just laughed. "You're looking for something and you'd better find it by Monday, isn't that right?"

Even Ben was impressed this time. His eyes opened wide with surprise.

Jeffrey pulled his hand back fast. "Did you see that on my hand?"

"No, your father told me," she said. "By the way, good luck, guys."

As Jeffrey and Ben left the tent, Ben said, "I told you all that stuff was baloney."

"You almost believed her," Jeffrey teased.

"No way," Ben argued, leading the way to the hot-dog grill area.

Ben chose their hot dogs scientifically, by smelling the smoke for the most perfect aroma. "A hot dog that smells good tastes good," he said.

That was how they had always picked their hot dogs, ever since they were little kids. Jeffrey was having so much fun that he almost forgot to worry about his dad's missing baseball cards.

They were eating their perfect hot dogs when they suddenly heard screams coming from the haunted house. The fifth-graders had created it by putting several tents together and making them as dark inside as possible. Then the fifth-graders hid in the dark corners of the tents, wearing masks and holding flashlights. When they wanted to scare kids, they flipped the flashlights on their masks and yelled.

Suddenly, Ben and Jeffrey saw Brian Carr run out of the haunted house as if he had jets on his sneakers.

"There's a ghost in there," Brian said as he ran by Jeffrey and Ben.

"Sure," Ben said. "And the goldfish in the penny-toss bowls are really sharks, too."

"No, I mean for real," Brian insisted. "I saw a ghost that was just a head. It had no body, and it was coming right at me and saying these weird things."

"What kind of weird things?" asked Jeffrey.

"It sounded like 'coolsville' and 'total gas,'" Brian said. "Then it asked me about my baseball cards. Is that weird or what?"

Jeffrey and Ben looked at each other. Now they knew that Brian was telling the truth— Max was there! But they weren't going to admit it to Brian.

"Come on, Brian," Jeffrey said. "Even you can make up a better story than that."

"I'm telling the truth," Brian said angrily.
"I saw a real ghost."

Ben and Jeffrey just laughed and walked
away. Everywhere the two best friends went,
they saw people having a great time. And one
of the big reasons was that Max was there,
turning the Fall Festival into what he would
call a "total gas."

Finally, Ben and Jeffrey decided to visit the
fishing booth. For one ticket they could throw
a fishing line over a high curtain. Mr. and Mrs.
Thompsen were hidden on the other side.
They stood there attaching small prizes to the
ends of the fishing poles.

But when Jeffrey and Ben threw their lines
over the curtain, Max was waiting on the other
side. He gave Jeffrey three prizes on one
hook: rubber snakes with glow-in-the-dark
tongues. And on Ben's line Max put a wad of
unused Fall Festival tickets.

But when Brian Carr reeled in his prize, he discovered that there was a real fish at the end of it! And in the fish's mouth was a baseball card. Brian took one look at the fish and ran off.

When it was Jeffrey's turn to stake out the baseball-card trading booth, he got his mind set for the job. He was a detective now, so he would have to start acting like a detective. He decided to check out the scene carefully, looking for suspects.

Jeffrey glanced around at the five tables set up in a semicircle. There were eight kids sitting there with their baseball cards, some in plastic pages, others just lying there in a heap.

Jeffrey tried to make himself invisible so that no one would notice that he was watching their every move.

"Hi, Jeffrey. What'cha doing?" asked Arvin Pubbler. He was standing right in front of Jeffrey, blocking the view of the tables and all of the baseball-card collections.

Jeffrey thought quickly. What would a real detective do now? He'd ask questions instead of answering them.

"What are you doing here, Arvin?" asked Jeffrey.

"I was just sort of walking around, you know? And this is where I ended up."

Jeffrey rolled his eyes. Detective or not, no one could get a sensible answer out of Arvin Pubbler. He tried to get away from Arvin so that he could spy on everyone. And he took seventeen pictures with Ben's soda-can camera. He even offered to make some big trades hoping to catch the baseball-card thief that way. But there wasn't much action. Most of the big card traders and collectors had gone home.

Late that afternoon, when the Fall Festival was over, Jeffrey met his friends again to walk home.

They were all full of hot dogs and popcorn. And their pockets were filled with the prizes they had won.

But the news from the baseball-card trading booth wasn't good. No one—not Jeffrey or Ben or Kenny or Ricky—had seen anyone or anything suspicious. They hadn't discovered one new clue to help them solve the case.

"A lot of kids had old cards, but not yours," Kenny reported. "I took a lot of pictures with Ben's camera."

So had everyone else when they were at the

booth. Ben was going to have the film developed by Monday morning.

"Well," Jeffrey said, "I'm glad I had some fun today, because the day after tomorrow is Monday. And unless those pictures reveal a surprise clue, I probably won't be having any more fun for a long, long time."

Chapter Six

Monday morning came much too soon. Jeffrey wasn't ready. He needed a clue, a suspect, or a miracle. Or at least he needed some last-minute help from Max!

Jeffrey made sure he got up, got dressed, and had breakfast before his father even rolled out of bed. Usually, having breakfast with his father was a lot of fun. The early morning was Jeffrey's favorite time to bring up dangerous school topics like report cards and detentions. Or dangerous at-home topics like articles of clothing that had mysteriously gotten jammed in the garage-door opener. In the early morning Mr. Becker was still pretty sleepy—or, as Jeffrey put it, "open to reason."

But not today. No way. Not this Monday. Jeffrey knew there could be only one topic of conversation on this particular Monday. It would be short and to the point: "It's Monday. Where are my baseball cards, Jeffrey?"

So Jeffrey left a note for his parents, and got out of the house before his father had a chance to say it. He went directly to Ben's house, where he found Ben in a corner of what Ben called his science lab. It was actually a corner of Ben's cluttered bedroom, but it was big enough for a table, which held Ben's science stuff. It was also far enough away from the rest of his family so that they wouldn't get blasted if one of Ben's experiments backfired.

"I was up really late last night developing the photos we took of people at the baseball-card trading booth," Ben said as Jeffrey entered his room.

"Great," Jeffrey said. "Let's see them."

Ben kept the pictures behind his back. "Before I show them to you, I want to remind you that a plan is only as good as the people who carry it out. We're not professional photographers."

Jeffrey was getting Ben's message loud and clear. It was written all over his worried face. "Okay, Ben, let's skip the speeches. What went wrong and how bad is it?"

In answer, Ben pulled out the photos.

Every photo taken at the booth had a big blur right in the middle of it. "I can't see anything," Jeffrey said. "What is that blur?"

"It's not exactly a blur," Ben said. "It's Arvin Pubbler."

"That's pretty close to being a blur," Jeffrey said with a sigh.

"Every time we tried to take a picture, Arvin just happened to get in the way," Ben said. "Sorry, Jeffrey. My plan washed out."

Jeffrey didn't know what to say, but he smiled at his friend, anyway.

"However, this doesn't mean we can't solve the case," Ben went on. "I've been doing some research about solving mysteries, and listen to this. Every crime case has three main parts to it."

"Yeah, a beginning, a middle, and an end," Jeffrey moaned. "And believe me, Ben, this is the end for me."

"Not necessarily." Ben stepped over to a chalkboard on the wall of his room. "Here are the three parts. First, *motive*—that means who wanted to steal your cards and why." He wrote the word *motive* on the board.

"Brian Carr doesn't like me," Jeffrey said. "Is that a good motive?"

Ben nodded.

"Of course, Gary McKane hates my guts. That's probably an even better motive, huh?"

Ben nodded again. Then he wrote down the second word. "*Means*—this means who knew how to steal the cards."

"I'll bet Brian knew how. He probably took a class in stealing—and Gary was probably his teacher."

Ben smiled and wrote down the third word. "*Opportunity*—who had a chance to steal the cards after Max left them on your desk."

"Hey, Daddy-os, did I hear my name? Like, don't talk about me behind my back," said the ghost. He came into sight with his back turned toward Jeffrey and Ben. Then he turned around with a sad face. "Come on, Jeffrey. How many times do I have to say sorrysville about leaving the cards on your desk?"

"I know you are, Max," Jeffrey said. "We were trying to figure out who took them."

Ben went on writing on the chalkboard. "We know that Gary was in the classroom and so was Brian," he said as he made Xs on a map of the school. "But who else had the opportunity to steal the cards?"

"Arvin Pubbler," said Max as he looked at the photos from the card-trading booth.

"Yeah, that's Arvin in the pictures," Jeffrey said.

"No, Daddy-o, I'm talking strictly opportunitysville," said the ghost. He floated over, picked up a piece of chalk, and drew another X in Ben's drawing. "Arvin was, like, here."

"That's the girls' bathroom," Ben pointed out.

The ghost quickly rubbed out the X. "I mean here . . . or somewhere. Like, forget the map. What I'm trying to tell you is that Arvin was in the nurse-erino's office. I happened to be there catching my afternoon z's on the cot and grooving on the warm cola the nurse keeps for the kids who get tummyaches. Well, just before I closed my eyes, Arvin came in. He was, like, moaning and telling the nurse that his stomach hurt. But meanwhile, back at the ranch, he was holding his head. I mean, this cat needs some lessons on how to pretend to be sick, right?"

"But, Max, I know Arvin went to the nurse's office," Jeffrey said. "We saw him leave music class. So what? He does it every week."

"Okay, Daddy-o. You're hip to everything, and I don't have to tell you about what Arvin was hiding in his shirt."

"*What* was he hiding in his shirt?" asked Ben.

"Beats me," said Max. "I didn't see. But I can guess. Maybe Arvin made like a leaf and fell by the classroom before he went to the nurse's office."

"Max, are you trying to say that maybe Arvin Pubbler stole my dad's baseball cards?" asked Jeffrey.

"I'm planting it. Are you digging it?"

"Yeah, but it's too unbelievable," Jeffrey said. "Arvin would never take anything that doesn't belong to him. In fact, he'd never take anything that *does* belong to him, either."

It was a long shot, but what else could Jeffrey do? He decided to set a trap to see if Arvin walked into it. Jeffrey asked to use Ben's phone, then called Arvin.

"Arvin Pubbler?" Jeffrey said, disguising his voice and trying to sound as grown-up as possible.

68

"Yes," said Arvin, obviously with a mouth full of breakfast cereal.

"I'm from the Board of Health Department," Jeffrey went on. "We've been calling lots of students your age to warn them."

"Warn them?" Arvin repeated with concern. "Warn them about what?"

Jeffrey knew the way to get Arvin's attention was to scare him—and almost everything scared him.

"It's about dangerous baseball cards. If you have purchased, received, or acquired any baseball cards, new or old, in the last seven days, you could be in major personal danger. There's a condition going around called Contaminated Baseball Cards. We've had a number of recent reports on it. If you've got it, your hands could come off and fall right into the sewer."

Jeffrey could hear Arvin breathing hard on the other end of the line. But what did it mean? Was Arvin getting nervous because he had stolen Jeffrey's cards? Or because he had always been afraid of sewers?

"What can I do?" Arvin said.

"If you have any baseball cards," Jeffrey continued, "bring them immediately to the corner of Brookridge and Elkmont. Someone will meet you there who will know what to do with you."

Jeffrey hung up before Arvin could ask any more questions. "Okay," he said to Ben and Max. "That's the best I can do. Let's go get the contamination squad and wait for Arvin."

A little later, Jeffrey, Ben, Melissa, Ricky, Kenny, and Max were taking up practically the entire sidewalk, waiting for Arvin to come. Luckily, he didn't keep them waiting long. He came jogging up to the corner with wide swatches of masking tape wrapped from his wrists to his shoulders.

"What's the tape for, Arvin?" asked Ricky.

"To keep my hands from falling off," Arvin said. "Did you guys get the call about Contaminated Baseball Cards?"

"We heard about it," said Melissa.

"I wonder who we're supposed to give our cards to," Arvin said.

"To me," answered Jeffrey.

Arvin began to reach into his backpack, then stopped. He stared at Jeffrey, who stared back hard.

Slowly, Arvin began to catch on. "There's

70

no Contaminated Baseball Cards, huh?" asked Arvin.

"Only stolen ones," Jeffrey said seriously.

Arvin's shoulders slumped as he handed Jeffrey his cards. Jeffrey quickly looked through them. One by one. One hundred and thirteen perfect baseball cards and each one at least thirty years old. Boy, they felt good in Jeffrey's hands.

"They're all there," Arvin said quietly. "I was careful with them."

"Yeah, but you stole them," Melissa said.

"I know," Arvin said. "I'm sorry, Jeffrey. I know I shouldn't have done it. I'm really sorry."

"Why did you?" Jeffrey asked coldly.

"You guys have great baseball cards, and I don't have many," Arvin said. He pulled nervously on a thread on his shirt. "And every time I wanted to see your cards, you guys told me I had to wash my hands or move to another state or something. You never let me see them." Arvin stared at the ground. "And would you trade cards with me? No way. Not with me. All you ever do is call me a wimp when you think I'm not listening."

71

Jeffrey and his friends looked at each other. No one looked very happy.

"And then Jeffrey got his dad's cards," Arvin went on. "I couldn't believe it. See, all my dad cares about is hockey. Hockey, hockey, and more hockey. He never had any baseball cards. He thought it was really cool when he showed me a hockey puck that's supposed to have some guy's blood on it."

"I'm sorry you don't have any good cards, Arvin," Jeffrey said. "I guess you felt pretty left out."

"Like, psst, Daddy-o." Max was whispering in Jeffrey's ear. He handed Jeffrey a stack of baseball cards. "Lay some of these cards on everyone—including Arvin. It's my own personal and grooviest collection," Max said. "See you later, alligator."

Then the ghost was gone.

Jeffrey took a quick flip through Max's cards. His eyes widened as he saw that they were just as old and perfect as his dad's.

"Uh, hey, you guys—and you, too, Arvin," Jeffrey said. "It just so happens that a friend of mine is giving away his collection of fabulous old baseball cards. And he wants us *all* to share them. Pretty radical, huh?" Jeffrey passed out the cards.

"I don't believe it," Kenny said. "You mean Max . . . ?"

Jeffrey cut him off fast. "The owner doesn't want his name mentioned. He just wanted us to know what a good friend he really is"—Jeffrey looked straight at Arvin—"to all of us."

Everyone loved the cards. And everyone had his or her own way of showing it.

Ben tested his cards to see if they were really old.

Ricky counted his to be sure he still had more than anyone else.

And Melissa studied the batting averages for a long time. "My batting average is still better," she declared.

Everyone was happy except Arvin.

"Arvin, what's your problem?" Ricky said. "You are holding in your hot little hands one heavy-duty classic-card collection."

"I know," Arvin said. "But there's something better that I've really really always always wanted."

"What's that?" Ricky asked.

"A complete collection of Skippy Lendler cards!" Arvin announced proudly.

Skippy Lendler? The worst player in the league? Jeffrey and his friends all rushed to get out their baseball cards.

"I'll trade with you, Arvin. Honest—any time!" everyone shouted at once.

It was the happiest day of Arvin Pubbler's life.

Here's a peek at Jeffrey's next adventure with Max, the fourth-grade ghost:

MAX'S SECRET FORMULA

"Max, we want to see the flying formula, don't we, Ben?" Jeffrey said.

Ben cautiously nodded his head.

"Like, all right!" said the ghost as he started picking out some chemicals from Ben's new chemistry set that he just received for Christmas. Then he looked around for something to pour them in. Suddenly he noticed a crystal vase on a nearby table that was shaped something like a bowl.

"Oh no! Not in there!" Ben shouted.

But it was too late. Max emptied two bottles of chemicals in it. Then he combined red and silver powders.

"Are you sure that stuff is supposed to bubble?" asked Ben.

"And smell so bad?" asked Jeffrey.

"If you think the smell is a drag, wait till you taste it!"

"Taste it!" Jeffrey said. "We're not going to drink that!"

"Well, Daddy-o, I can pour it on you, but like you won't dig what happens then."

"What will happen?" asked Ben.

Max picked up the bowl and swirled the dark steaming liquid. "Haven't you cats ever heard of the Wolfman and Dracula?"

ABOUT THE AUTHORS

Bill and Megan Stine have written many books and stories for young readers including several in these series: *The Three Investigators*; *Wizards, Warriors, and You*; and *Find Your Fate: Indiana Jones*. They live in Atlanta, Georgia, with their son, Cody.